THE BIBLE IN THE WALL

Translated from the German
By
H.J.D

Grace & Truth Books

Sand Springs, Oklahoma

ISBN# 1-58339-053-7
First printings, 1800's (date unknown)
Second printing, Triangle Press, 1993
Third printing, Grace & Truth Books, 2003

Cover art by Caffy Whitney
Cover layout by Ben Gundersen

Grace & Truth Books
3406 Summit Boulevard
Sand Springs, Oklahoma   74063

Phone: 918 245 1500
www.graceandtruthbooks.com
email: gtbooksorders@cs.com

TABLE of CONTENTS

I'll build it in the wall.

Chapter One

ANTONIO AND HIS BIBLE

In the beginning of the summer in 1856 a young bricklayer named Antonio, who was full of life and fun, left his home in the Swiss Canton of Tessin (on today's maps it is called Tecino) to look for work. The young man packed his tools and clothes into a bundle which he carried on a stick over his shoulder. He hiked over the mountains to German Switzerland.

As he walked along the mountainous trail, he met a lady. She spoke to him and gave him an Italian Bible. She begged him to read the Book because it was the Word of God. She said it pointed out the way to everlasting life.

Antonio took the gift hesitatingly. He didn't thank her, but he did push it into his bundle as he went on his way. Some troubling thoughts entered into his mind. His village priest had often warned him of the dangers in Protestant countries. The priest told Antonio and his friends not to read the "soul-destroying books of the heretics."

During this time in history much distrust took place among the various religions. Most people of that part of the world had long belonged to the Roman Catholic Church. A Roman Catholic priest named Martin Luther had come to understand the doctrines of the Bible differently from his church.

Martin Luther began to protest against the teaching of the Catholic Church; therefore, the Roman Catholic Church called Luther and his followers protesters. We call those churches who follow the teaching of Martin Luther, "Protestants," even today.

Most of the priests he knew had warned Antonio against the Bible. They told Antonio the Bible was very dangerous for the unlearned and that reading the Bible had deceived even Martin Luther, a Catholic priest! Now Antonio carried that "dangerous book" in his bundle. Antonio decided he would get rid of the Bible as soon as possible. In doubt as to whether to throw it away at once or to wait for a better opportunity, he decided to wait. The young man walked on until he reached the lovely little Swiss town of Glarus. Antonio soon found work there with others he knew from his home town.

Antonio worked on a fine, new building. One day while laying the bricks, he came to a gap in the wall. He had to put something in that gap. Suddenly, a clever idea came to his mind; he would fill the gap with the Bible that he had no desire to keep. "And," he exclaimed, laughing, "we'll see whether the devil will get it out again in a hurry!"

Antonio's home town friends who worked with him thought his idea wonderful and amusing; so Antonio did it. He took the Book out of his bundle and tried to force the Bible into the gap. He gave it two or three hard blows with his hammer. These blows made deep dents in the cover. His friends roared with laughter while Antonio forced the Bible into the opening and covered it up with mortar.

Winter drew near. The brickwork on the building was finished, so the workers began to think about going home. Most of the men didn't have much money left from all their work because they had wasted most of their wages on drinking.

Traveling across the Alps.

Chapter Two
THE WILD SOUTH WIND

Now, five years later, let us look at the town of Glarus again. It lays nearly in the center of beautiful Switzerland on the Linth River. Glarus has grown into a rich, busy town of 4,000 people. A row of fine brick buildings line Main Street. Most of the people earn money by working in one of the many nearby factories. Steam or the strong current of the river powers the machinery in these factories. The town is in a valley with splendid green meadows that go up the slopes of the mountains on both sides of the valley. The cheerful, sunny peak of Mt. Shilt rises on the east side of the valley. From the southwest the gigantic, gloomy, rocky mass of Mt. Glarnisch looms above the town.

This beautiful spot, with all the charms and grandeur of a Swiss landscape, also bitterly experiences the terror nature can cause. The Linth River flows from south to north through the valley. Glarus is at the north end of this valley. Fierce winds often follow the same path as the river. The people dread these winds and storms which they call *Der wilde Foehn* (wild south wind). These winds give warning of their coming in several ways. Sometimes the people hear a strange roaring up among the mountains. A wild rustling moves through the forests. At last, like water bursting from a broken dam, the raging storm roars through the high valleys. Then it casts itself howling into the lower canyons. Roofs fly off the houses. The wild wind tears trees up by their roots. It tears pieces of rock from the steep mountain sides and hurls them into the canyon below. Suddenly, it will become very still. Then the storm will rage with even more force. After a few days, the storm will blow itself out. Then the north winds will bring rain.

These days of danger for our charming town of Glarus may return ten or twelve times a year. The people know the danger. For hundreds of years they have enforced very strict laws while this wild *Foehn* rages. All workmen who use fire in their business must stop working and put out their fires. Blacksmiths and locksmiths put out their fires at the first signs of a storm. The town allows no lights to burn in the factories. Steam engines sit idle. The townspeople must put out all lights and fires in their houses; no one can bake bread. In some places, no one may even cook. Shooting is forbidden. Special watchmen walk the street to see that the people obey the laws.

What had preserved Glarus for centuries from destruction by fire? Was it because the people obeyed these laws, or was it because of the merciful and kind protection of God? In the years 1299 and 1337 fire reduced Glarus to ashes. Again in 1477 they suffered much from a fire. For the last four hundred years, however, Glarus had escaped any hurt. It is no wonder then that many people thought the rules were old-fashioned and unnecessary.

On Ascension-day, May 9, 1861, the town of Glarus held a *Landsgemeinde*. A *Landsgemeinde* is a gathering of all the men of the land who can vote and use a gun. The meeting took place outside, and the men considered and carried out all public business for their local area.

Warm and serious debates about taxes, forest-laws, street and school matters went on at this time. Some of the men also asked about ending the fire laws. They said the laws had become old-fashioned and placed hardships on the businesses. After talking about the good and the bad affects of the fire laws, most of the men thought they should keep the old laws. Therefore, they did not make any changes in the old fire laws.

Chapter Three

THE FIRE

The very next day, Friday, May 10, the *Foehn* gave warning of its coming. The well-known signs did not frighten the people. So on Friday night almost everyone went to bed as usual, except a few who enjoyed staying up late to visit with friends.

Suddenly between nine and ten o'clock at night, they heard the cry of "Fire!" Flames burst forth from the stable. No one knew how or why the fire started in the stable because no one used fire there. Firemen rushed to the stable from all directions. The fire was already burning in three or four places.

The *Foehn* grew stronger, and it drove the flames with the speed of lightning. The firemen stopped the flames from going farther west, but not before the roof of the druggist's house burst into flames. While the firemen stopped the flames on the roof, the fire moved farther and farther north. That was the direction the *Foehn* was blowing.

The fire spread to the roofs of many buildings. The wind carried flaming bits of the burning roofs. New fires started and spread wherever they fell. In half an hour the flames had leaped to hundreds of roofs in the town.

Many men came to the stable to fight the fire. When they saw the fire spread toward their own homes, the men ran back home with fear and despair. Often they arrived just in time to rescue their dear ones. Some saved most of their valuables, but they could not save their homes.

"No human imagination," says a reporter, "can form a picture of that terrible hour. The confusion, noise, and terror are beyond description. Who can paint such a scene?" said the reporter as he watched the dreadful, crackling flames. The firemen struggled desperately against the flames as long as possible. At last, for their own safety's sake, they abandoned their engines or pushed them into the stream.

"You can only imagine the noise of the howling storm," the reporter said, "as one listened to the loud cries of the women and children running for safety. Add to this the roaring of the ever growing sea of fire! What a terrifying scene!"

Amid the fury of the storm and the weakness of man, He could and did in His mercy send help. Who is He? He is the God of heaven "Who maketh his angels spirits; his ministers a flaming fire," Psalms 104:4. In spite of all this noise, the other villages did not hear the ringing of the fire bell. The glow of the fires lit up Mount Glarnisch all the way to the top. This glow told the nearby villages of the terrible calamity. Not one of these villages had enough fire engines or other means of putting out

The fire engines are coming.

such a fire. Oh, if they could only get help from Zurich or from the big towns on the lake!

In vain the faithful officer in charge of the telegraph stayed on the job. In spite of the thick smoke and the heat of the fire, he sent many messages begging for help to Schwanden, to Uznach, and to Zurich. No one answered.

In 1861 the Swiss telegraph did not operate at night. Nevertheless, the Glarus operator tried one last time before the flames forced him to leave. He telegraphed his desperate message to Rapperswil. In God's providence the clerk there had stayed late. To his great surprise, he heard the warning on the wire and soon read the terrible words: "Fire! fire! a dreadful fire! help! speedy help!"

The clerk immediately gave the alarm. In a very little while a special train with firemen and fire engines rushed to Glarus. They arrived at daybreak in time to rescue some of those fine buildings on Main Street.

Shortly after, trains bringing more fire engines and more men arrived from Zurich, Wadenswil, and Sargans. A great battle followed. Human power, skill, and judgment battled on the one side, and the blind fury of nature fought on the other side. The firemen saved the factories which the people of Glarus credited for their living. The firemen put up a barrier which the fire could not pass. The wind calmed, and the fire had nothing more to devour.

On Saturday morning over half of the town of Glarus lay buried in ashes and ruins. A dark smoke hung over the whole village. Now and then one could hear hissing tongues of fire. Four hundred ninety buildings lay in ashes. Most of the public buildings were gone. Three hundred homes had burned. The well-to-do villagers suffered the most; they lost everything.

As you will remember, the people of Glarus had talked about ending the fire laws the night before the fire started. They had decided to keep the ancient laws, but they placed their faith in their wisdom instead of God's grace and mercy. The people forgot to thank God for His protecting care. That night fire started in the stable even though the stable hands never used fire when they worked.

However, the flames that destroyed Glarus kindled the love spoken of by Jesus in the second great commandment. Jesus said in Matthew 22:39, "And the second is like unto it, Thou shalt love thy neighbour as thyself." A wonderful, practical, and generous love glowed in the hearts of the Swiss people toward each other. Help of all kinds streamed to their brothers in distress. Food, clothing, household furniture, tools, and large sums of money came from throughout the whole country. Many of the most wealthy and able men of the land came with advice and help.

The kindness of others provided shelter and the necessary things of life for the homeless. The people spent the whole summer and following winter clearing away the rubbish and litter. They also drew plans for new buildings. The work started as soon as the swallows returned in the spring of 1862. Troops of workmen, masons, and carpenters came to the spot where Glarus had stood. They began to build a finer and larger town on the ashes.

Chapter Four

FINDING THE BIBLE

Most of the masons who worked in the central and southern parts of Switzerland lived in the Canton of Tessin and nearby in the northern part of Italy. In the spring, groups of men made their way over the mountains to help rebuild Glarus. They carried a few clothes and tools in red bundles on their shoulders. When winter approached, they would wander back home again. Some of the men saved most of their wages. The money saved would keep their families through the winter.

One group of twelve men crossed the mountains to seek work in Glarus. The younger lads played pranks and told jokes. These lively young men eagerly looked forward to seeing a new country, different people, and new customs. Often they broke out into their favorite Italian songs. Mario, one of the young men, frequently took a book out of his pocket. He tried to read parts of his book aloud to the others every time they stopped to rest. He told them how important the contents of his book were.

Mario was an Italian from Genoa. Once a Roman Catholic, he was now an excited member of a free, evangelical church. The book Mario read with such feeling to his companions was the New Testament. He had recently discovered the deadly errors of teaching salvation by works. But alas! He did not really understand the living truth of the gospel of salvation by grace. This is the point in doctrine where Martin Luther differed with the Catholic church.

When Mario talked to his traveling companions, he often made them angry because he would attack the Pope. He tried to make the Pope appear ridiculous rather than proclaim the sweet truth of the free grace of God in Christ. Young Mario didn't realize that rather than teaching the Spirit of Christ during the journey, his ridicule caused bitterness.

One of the men in this group of travelers was often quiet and thoughtful. He seemed to take much pleasure in listening to his young companion. Giovanni was an older man, between fifty and sixty years of age. He didn't joke or sing or laugh with the others. He was very sad. He was lonely for his wife and children whom he had left at home alone. Giovanni left home to travel to Glarus for six or eight months of hard work because his family needed the money. He hoped he could save enough for his beloved family to get through the winter. These thoughts gave Giovanni the courage to go forward.

Giovanni had another special reason for listening with such attention and pleasure to the reading of the Testament. At home a Christian lady had given him a copy of this very Book. His priest had demanded the Book. Giovanni gave it up

Finding the Bible.

without any fuss because he didn't realize its value. He was sorry now that he had acted so cowardly.

At last the journey ended. The men had crossed the mountains, and they had come to the town of Glarus. Although they did not all work on the same building, all of the men immediately found work. Giovanni worked rebuilding a house. Some of the walls of the house still stood, but before they started rebuilding, the workers checked the strength of these walls. Were they strong and solid enough to use as part of the new building? The workers hit the walls with heavy blows to test their strength.

"This was almost a new house," said Giovanni to one of the workmen who worked under him. "It can't be over five or six years old. Look how the fire burnt the inside of the house to ashes, but these bricks are still in good condition. Some of them sound quite hollow. Let's see how far the damage goes." Upon this, he swung his pick-ax in the air. He brought it down with great force, and he knocked out several bricks. To everyone's surprise, a book fell to the ground.

Giovanni picked it up. With amazement and pleasure, he exclaimed, "A Bible!"

The workmen crowded around him to see the wonderful Book with their own eyes. Giovanni, with a tiny shudder, opened the Book and read aloud the first words that met his eyes. From Proverbs 12:2 he read, "A good man obtaineth favour of the Lord: but a man of wicked devices will he condemn."

"Oh! how happy I am," he exclaimed, clasping the Book with an expression of deep thankfulness. "How I have longed for a Bible. I know I don't deserve this wonderful gift. Once before a lady gave one to me. Our priest asked for it, and I foolishly gave it to him. This time—I'll die before I'll give the Bible up!"

Most of the Italians who surrounded Giovanni and saw his emotion did not know how to read. So they didn't argue with him about keeping the Book. The wonder of how the Book got there interested the men far more than keeping the Book. The men carefully examined the wall from which it fell. They decided someone had placed the Book in the wall on purpose. They saw the three deep dents on the cover. Someone had also damaged the Book with several blows on purpose. Even so, with a heart full of joy Giovanni took the Bible as a gift from the hand of God.

From this time forward, Giovanni read the Book every day whenever he had free time. On Sundays he gathered friends and read aloud from parts of the Book for them. The story of his discovery of the Bible soon spread. Many people came out of curiosity to see the Book. At this time Giovanni had little understanding of the Word of God, so he couldn't explain what he read. His ignorance of God's Word reminds us of what we read in Acts 8:30-31, "And Philip ran thither to him, and heard him read the prophet Esaias, and said, Understandest thou what thou readest? And he said,

How can I, except some man should guide me? And he desired Philip that he would come up and sit with him."

Giovanni wisely began to read from the New Testament because it is easier to understand. Gradually, he began to refer to the Old Testament. Then he learned to pray by reading the Book of Psalms. What Jesus said of the Holy Ghost, "He shall glorify me: for he shall receive of mine, and shall shew it unto you," John 16:14, proved true for Giovanni.

The Holy Spirit showed Giovanni the blessed truths of Christ; then he taught those who came to listen. As they moved forward step by step in the Scriptures, the Holy Spirit gave them more light.

This did not stop others, however, from showing bitterness, making rude insults, and finally threats against Giovanni and his friends. All of these actions could have frightened and discouraged our friend Giovanni, for he had not yet come to understand the gospel of Jesus Christ in Luke 6:22-23, "Blessed are ye, when men shall hate you, and when they shall separate you from their company, and shall reproach you, and cast out your name as evil, for the Son of man's sake. Rejoice ye in that day, and leap for joy: for, behold, your reward is great in heaven: for in the like manner did their fathers unto the prophets."

One day a Swiss evangelist visited the place where Giovanni worked. He met Giovanni and encouraged him to look to Christ by faith. He showed Giovanni the blessings of being hated because he taught God's Word. The evangelist also gave Giovanni some good advice. He advised Giovanni to set up a free school in the hut where the workers lived. In his free time Giovanni could teach reading, writing, and arithmetic. The school would interest those who fought against him and win their hearts. He might also use his Bible for teaching them to read.

Giovanni willingly agreed and joyfully set to work. At first a large number came to learn. Tired from their day's work, some found it hard to study; others stayed and completed their lessons. Those who finished the classes received a lovely gift! A lady, who worked with the Swiss evangelist, gave each one an Italian New Testament.

Soon the value of Giovanni's efforts began to show. The workers who learned to read were reading their own New Testaments! They also learned to write and do arithmetic. By this new skill they found that dishonest builders cheated them out of much of their wages when paying them. The workers could now go over their own accounts and figure out what they had earned.

Another exciting benefit came to light. What joy filled the men when they could read letters from the families they had left behind! With much gladness the workers could now write letters to their loved ones at home.

Oh, how many ways we can serve others with love. Love to God and to His Holy Word had taught

Giovanni, the new school master, to serve his fellowman in love. As Giovanni served his fellow workers, he learned too, and became a better teacher. Because of the service of love Giovanni showed the workers, they did not close their hearts when he talked about spiritual matters to them. Now Giovanni could teach them the basic truths of godliness and did so with more clearness and ability. Only God knows the full effect all this had on the souls of Giovanni's students.

Chapter Five

GIOVANNI AND THE PRIEST

The masonry work proceeded rapidly during the warm and dry summer of 1862. Giovanni began to look forward to the day when he would turn his steps toward home. He had managed to save a precious sum of money from his labor. At last November came with its short days. The Italian workers were anxious to leave, and on one of the early days of November they set off. Our friend, Giovanni, could hardly wait for the day when he would again see his dear wife and children.

Snow storms had already arrived in the mountains. That made crossing them dangerous. The danger only added to Giovanni's joy when he reached home safely. To the delight of his children he carefully removed from his bundle a small gift for each one.

Sorrow mixed with joy at Giovanni's reunion with his family. His loving wife, Gina, had suffered a severe fall and broke her arm during his absence. She had slipped as she carried a sack of chestnuts down the steep hill into town. Because the village had no doctor to set and care for Gina's broken bone, the poor woman's arm hung useless by her side. It remained useless for the rest of her life.

This was a bitter cup for Giovanni. He was saddened by his wife's injury. However, he still remembered with thanks that the Lord had prospered his labor that summer. The money from his work would buy a goat and provide for the family all winter. His family had harvested an abundant crop of hay and chestnuts during his absence. With God's blessing they would suffer no want.

During the long winter evenings Giovanni had many things to tell to his family and friends. He talked about the fire of Glarus and God's wonderful providences. He told how God had helped many to escape danger. He told of God's providing hand in many instances for the people of Glarus. He told them about the manners and customs of the Swiss people. He told stories about his dangerous journey over the mountains and how God spared him.

The most important story this father told his family was the strange tale of the Bible's discovery. Giovanni never tired of telling it. All the neighbors came to hear the wonderful story with their own ears and to see this strange Book with their own eyes. Most who came wanted to hear something read out of the Book, and Giovanni gladly read the Bible to them.

Soon these simple people began to feel that what was read to them was most beautiful. They learned, and more easily understood the Word of God, through Giovanni's direct reading from the Bible than from the Latin mass and the dull sermons of their priest. It was no wonder that Giovanni's small house filled every evening with neighbors and friends. These people longed and thirsted for salvation! Jesus says in Matthew 5:6, "Blessed are they which do hunger and thirst after righteousness: for they shall be filled."

One day a visitor, whom Giovanni had expected, knocked on the door. It was the priest. He wanted to see this much-talked about Bible without delay. "Certainly you shall, Sir," answered Giovanni, "but under one condition: you may not take the Book from me, for God Himself has given me this Bible."

"Blockhead," cried the priest. "You don't know the harm such a Book does when it falls into the hands of people in your station in life!"

This time Giovanni stood firm. Remember, dear reader, he had given in to the priest once before, and by doing so he had lost his New Testament. The people of Italy had full religious liberty now, and Giovanni knew this. The priests could not make the people obey the rules of the Catholic Church anymore.

The priest threatened Giovanni with excommunication from the church. Giovanni's wife and children became terrified as the priest threatened him with all the horrors of eternal damnation. This time Giovanni refused to give up his Bible. He knew that God had given him the precious volume. The priest left without Giovanni's Bible.

Chapter Six

THE BIBLE STALL

Ever since the dawn of religious liberty for the people in Italy, several Bible societies in England and France had taken advantage of this time of freedom. Perhaps this religious liberty would not last long, so they quickly spread the Divine Word throughout the whole country by sending out "Bible colporteurs." Colporteurs are sellers of goods.

One of these colporteurs heard of Giovanni's zeal and love for the Word of God. He had heard of Giovanni's stand against the priest. The colporteur told the Bible society friends who sent him out about Giovanni. They immediately asked Giovanni if he would like to join them for a few weeks and become a Bible-seller in Lombardy.

We must remember that Giovanni had by no means left the Catholic Church. While he read his Bible with excitement, he still went to mass regularly and took part in all the ceremonies of the Roman Catholic Church. Giovanni had been taught since childhood to be a good Catholic. While he saw a precious beauty in Scriptures he had never seen before, he could not give up all he had been taught from his youth in such a short time. He had not yet come to a clear understanding of the truth. Also, he had little or no chance to talk with other Christians who read the Bible.

Giovanni in the marketplace.

The idea of becoming a Bible-seller delighted Giovanni. In spite of the fears of his wife and the threats of his priest, he went to sell Bibles. He set off after a few days with a pack of Bibles and Testaments on his back.

A colporteur lives a difficult life, going from town to town, and stopping at each small village. At first Giovanni sold his Bibles very quickly. People kindly welcomed him wherever he went, especially in the towns. Giovanni usually put up his stall in the marketplace and offered his very uncommon goods for sale. He began with simplicity and sincerity to tell the people how great his Books were. The people eagerly listened, and his courage grew. One day he boldly decided to take his Bibles to Lugano, the capital of the Swiss Canton of Tessin. He knew Switzerland did not have the freedom to sell Bibles like Italy did, but he had many friends there whom he had met when working in Glarus. He decided to try to sell the Bible in Switzerland. Bravely Giovanni ventured forth.

Giovanni arrived on the yearly market day. The table on which he arranged his Bibles soon became surrounded by curious people. Most of these people did not approve of Giovanni trying to sell Bibles. Their feelings toward this kindly colporteur were more likely to be bad than good. Giovanni began gently urging those gathered around his table to buy the Word of God. He pointed out the low cost of the Bibles and showed the beautiful bindings of the Books. Giovanni told the people gathered around him what blessings the precious Book contained.

A young man in the crowd came up to him. He told Giovanni he could get a Bible for nothing if he wanted one. He boasted that he had plastered one up in a wall in Glarus five or six years ago. Surely, in spite of the fire, the devil had not been able to get it out again!

Much astonished and moved, Giovanni looked the man in the face. After a short pause, he replied, "Yes, that is true. In spite of the fire, that Bible received great care—it was saved almost by a miracle!"

Giovanni told the young man how God (not Satan) had permitted the precious Book to fall into his hands. He told how finding the Bible richly blessed him and afterwards many others. Now it was the young man's turn to be surprised.

"What!" cried Antonio, "you mean to say you have found the Bible that I put in the wall at Glarus? Let me see the Book! From the dents I made in the cover, I will know it anywhere."

Giovanni took his beloved Bible from his pocket and handed it to Antonio. Shocked and surprised, Antonio stared in disbelief at the Book! He thought he had placed that Book beyond the reach of any human being.

"Besides," Giovanni continued, "every man that worked with me last summer in Glarus can tell you the same story. Come now, young man, buy the

Bible from me. Do not hide it this time. Read it and learn from it how to be saved from your sins."

"Go away with your Bibles," cried Antonio. The old hatred towards this Holy Book was renewed and gained control of his heart. "We will have nothing to do with them. Who, I should like to know, has given you permission to come here?" With that he threw down the Bible. Turning to the crowd, Antonio stirred them up against our poor colporteur. Before Giovanni knew what had happened, they overturned his table and began hitting and kicking him. The crowd did not rest until he and his Bibles left Lugano.

With a heavy heart Giovanni turned toward home to recover from his wounds and bruises. He gave a careful account of the sale of his Bibles to those who had hired him. The winter season had passed and spring had arrived. Giovanni soon took up his hammer and trowel and bid farewell to his home. Once more he began the long journey over the mountains for a summer job.

Chapter Seven

ANTONIO IN THE HOSPITAL

God is most patient and long-suffering to those whom He will save. He is not hindered by pride nor arrogance. It is truly astonishing above all measure how He saves those who are bent on their own destruction.

Twice Antonio, the rough bricklayer from Tessin, rudely and wickedly refused to accept the same Bible. God had decreed to use this very Bible as a means to draw Antonio unto Himself and make him eternally happy.

For the third time this untiring, compassionate, loving God will cross Antonio's path. Again God will use the same Bible with the dented cover. Jesus says in Revelation 3:20, "Behold, I stand at the door, and knock: if any man hear my voice, and open the door, I will come in to him, and will sup with him, and he with me." Jesus kept knocking on the door of Antonio's heart with this same Bible!

Our now aged Giovanni had again found work in one of the Swiss towns. He soon found that the stubborn troublemaker, Antonio, not only worked in the same town but also on the same building. Antonio felt uncomfortable at first, especially when he saw how the other men treated Giovanni with

The Bible returned to Antonio a third time.

great respect. Giovanni was a foreman over all the Italian workmen.

Gradually, Antonio began to feel more regard and even some affection for his foreman, Giovanni. He anxiously wanted to have Giovanni forget the ill-treatment he had received at Lugano—ill-treatment pushed by Antonio. Giovanni willingly forgot the past and began to take a great interest in the young man.

One day as Antonio carried a heavy piece of stone up one of the unsteady ladders, his foot slipped. Perhaps weakness caused by his heavy drinking helped lead to his fall. · Antonio fell backwards from a height of about fifty feet. His fellow workers carried an unconscious Antonio to the little hospital in the town where the Sisters of Charity cared for him.

Poor young man, there he lay for weeks and months on a bed of suffering. Remember what God said to His people when He said He would send His chastening hand upon them for their sin. "For I know the thoughts that I think toward you, saith the Lord, thoughts of peace, and not of evil, to give you an expected end. Then shall ye call upon me, and ye shall go and pray unto me, and I will hearken unto you. And ye shall seek me, and find me, when ye shall search for me with all your heart," Jeremiah 29:11-13.

Giovanni often visited Antonio in the little hospital. Before the fall, Giovanni had warned Antonio against his sinful way of life. He had reminded Antonio of the certainty of God's chastening hand if he continued in sin. Now with tenderness and love Giovanni pointed the unhappy man to the Good Shepherd. Until people have been drawn to Christ, they are as Jesus said, "...they fainted, and were scattered abroad, as sheep having no shepherd," Matthew 9:36.

It was God who sent Giovanni to Antonio to tell him that God used chastening in love to bring His wandering sheep to Himself. Jesus says in Matthew 9:37-38, "The harvest truly is plenteous, but the labourers are few; Pray ye therefore the Lord of the harvest, that he will send forth labourers into his harvest." We must pray for God to send more to labor in His vineyard who will be honest with our souls like Giovanni.

Giovanni didn't stay long when he came to visit. Work began at four o'clock in the morning and did not end until nightfall. This left him little time or strength at his age to visit the sick. He wanted to do something more for poor Antonio, so he left him his old, precious Bible. Giovanni left the Bible on the condition that Antonio would read it and would take the best possible care of it.

Antonio did not care a bit about the Book. In fact the Bible laying on the table beside him made him feel angry. One day, however, Antonio picked it up when he was bored. He didn't read it; he just turned the pages for something to do. Some godly ladies, who came to visit him often, saw him just turning the pages to pass his time away. They told him about the twelfth chapter of Hebrews. They told Antonio that this chapter speaks about the blessings of suffering and how God sends suffering out of love. It tells about the love of God which reveals itself in a special way in chastening.

These words caught Antonio's attention. They soothed his dark and aching heart. As his eyes fell on the fifth verse these precious truths struck his heart, "And ye have forgotten the exhortation which speaketh unto you as unto children, My son, despise not thou the chastening of the Lord, nor faint when thou art rebuked of him." He read Verses 6-7, "For whom the Lord loveth he chasteneth, and scourgeth every son whom he receiveth. If ye endure chastening, God dealeth with you as with sons; for what son is he whom the father chasteneth not?"

The mystery of what Giovanni told him became clear. Now Antonio understood how God sent sore affliction in love to bring His wandering sheep to Himself.

Antonio's heart of rebellion melted as he read, "Now no chastening for the present seemeth to be joyous, but grievous: nevertheless afterward it yieldeth the peaceable fruit of righteousness unto them which are exercised thereby. Wherefore lift up the hands which hang down, and the feeble knees; And make straight paths for your feet, lest that which is lame be turned out of the way; but let it rather be healed. Follow peace with all men, and holiness, without which no man shall see the Lord," Hebrews 12:11-14.

From this time on Antonio read the Bible often, especially the passages his Christian friends suggested. Sometimes they gave him clear explanations of these passages. Slowly Antonio began to make progress in the knowledge of Christ and the things of God. He grew in love to the Word of God itself.

At first Antonio had hoped to regain his health and leave the hospital within six weeks. That did not happen. Six months passed before he could set a foot on the floor or even drag himself around the room on crutches. His hip had been broken in the fall, and the injury crippled him for life. Antonio's Christian friends told him he could never go back to work as a mason. He would need to find a different way to earn a living. His friends suggested that perhaps as he healed and had less pain, he could study. If he could increase his general knowledge enough, he might become a teacher. Antonio took their advice. He studied with great enthusiasm. He made rapid progress in many useful subjects. His desire for spiritual things also increased every day.

At length he gained the deepest and most important knowledge a man can get. He learned that he was a great sinner who deserved eternal judgment. The more the Holy Spirit opened his eyes to see the beauty there is in Christ, the more he could understand what Paul said in 1 Timothy 1:15, "This is a faithful saying, and worthy of all acceptation, that Christ Jesus came into the world to save sinners; of whom I am chief." Even the prophet Isaiah said,

"Then said I, Woe is me! for I am undone; because I am a man of unclean lips, and I dwell in the midst of a people of unclean lips: for mine eyes have seen the King, the Lord of hosts." Isaiah 6:5.

The more Antonio learned of God's wrath upon his sin, the more he saw his need for the blood of Jesus Christ to atone for it. He learned to see that he needed Christ's blood to cleanse him from sin, as well as His sacrifice to take away the penalty of sin.

Antonio learned the publican's prayer in Luke 18:13, "And the publican, standing afar off, would not lift up so much as his eyes unto heaven, but smote upon his breast, saying, God be merciful to me a sinner." What joy sprang up in Antonio's soul when he found that the Son of God could cleanse even such a sinner as he from all sin. From this time forward he experienced peace and joy. Antonio kept these feelings of peace in spite of his suffering. He even could thank God for the suffering which God used to bring him to Himself.

Chapter Eight

CONCLUSION

In the autumn of 1863 Antonio was released from the hospital. He did not return to Tessin because it was not yet open to the Word of God. He became a teacher in a Christian school in Italy.

Antonio worked as a schoolmaster in a little town surrounded by villages where several Christian families lived. The town had no schoolhouse, so Antonio taught the children in his home twice a week. He gave the children lessons and exercises to do at home. The children could only study in their free time. Free time for these children meant time when they were not working in the fields to help their parents.

In the meantime Antonio spent his free days holding meetings in the neighborhood. He wanted to spread the knowledge of the Word of God. With a cane he could walk short distances. Since his conversion, he led a sober and godly life, and his health improved greatly.

We still must look in on Giovanni. He has given his eldest daughter permission to marry a young schoolmaster. His name was Antonio, the same person who had hid the Bible in the wall. The changes in the young man had pleased Giovanni. Both Giovanni's wife and children have received the truth from God's Word. They have renounced serving the kingdom of darkness. Giovanni has promised that at his death, the Bible he found in the wall shall become the property of his son-in-law. Of course, Antonio can never look at the precious Bible with the dents struck into the cover without the color rushing to his cheeks.

Meanwhile, Giovanni finds his greatest pleasure lies in reading his precious Book. It is from this Book that he learns every day more about the grace and mercy which delivered him from chains of error and superstition. From his Bible he became especially aware of false teaching which leads to claiming salvation without true repentance.

Antonio has learned to see why God's Word always places repentance before remission of sins as we see in Mark 1:4, "John did baptize in the wilderness, and preach the baptism of repentance for the remission of sins."

The Bible has taught him to "worship God in spirit and in truth." We cannot please God in outward forms and useless ceremonies. The ceremonies of man cannot satisfy the craving of a hungry and thirsting soul. Now Giovanni and Antonio have found the blessedness of Christ-centered fellowship spoken of in Hebrews 10:24-25, "And let us consider one another to provoke unto love and to good works: Not forsaking the assembling of ourselves together, as the manner of some is; but exhorting one another: and so much the more, as ye see the day approaching."

The Lord said to the women of Samaria in John 4:23-24, "But the hour cometh, and now is, when the true worshippers shall worship the Father in spirit and in truth: for the Father seeketh such to worship him. God is a Spirit: and they that worship him must worship him in spirit and in truth."

THE BIBLE

'...thou hast magnified thy word above all thy flame," Psalms 138:2.

What must I think, or what believe,
And what must now my refuge be?
On every side they would deceive,
And take God's blessed Word from me;
And yet man's life is pain and woe,
In this his pilgrimage below.

One makes a pen to suit his hand,
Applies the knife, now here, now there;
But that God's Word, who all things planned,
Should be so handled anywhere,
Is that indeed which should surprise
An age like this, reputed wise.

The Book of books, th' Eternal Word,
Which God's own Spirit gave to me,
Is, in these times, by ways unheard,
Attack'd by infidelity;
And Satan's craft, in this our age,
Obtains more conquests than his rage.

For boasted reason sits enthroned,
And intellect's pretensions high
Have well-nigh Deity disowned,
And hurled defiance at the sky;

Planting their shafts of wit and sense
Against Thy truth, Omnipotence!

Oh! if what these Enlightened say,
About my hope in God most just;
And they could reason all away
My shelter, confidence, and trust;
And make God's Word a seeming lie,
And revelation quite deny!

What must I think, what must I do,
For peace or comfort anywhere?
If what the skeptic says is true,
I've trusted visions light as air.
If Moses wrote untruths on earth,
What can his song in heaven be worth?

Away, deceivers! mark it well,
Ye boast a mission pure and wise;
It needs no skill or wit to tell,
Nor should it cause the least surprise,
That Satan, who man's ruin sought.
Would Revelation set at nought.

The Bible teaches man to fear
The very God who gave him breath;
To love his neighbour far and near;
Commands the conscience, "Thus God saith!"
Tells of man's ruin to his face,
And shews a remedy in grace.

41

Thrice welcome is my precious Book!—
My Bible!--thousand-fold more dear!—
It bids me hope, and upward look
To regions pure, and bright, and clear;
Where the redeem'd walk in and out,
Without a conflict or a doubt.

And for believers there is rest,--
A long eternal Sabbath-day;
Secure in Jesus, fully blest,
Himself the Light, the Life, the Way;
There shall we hear our God proclaim
His Word is higher than His Name.

The Harvest Home

By Hannah More

The Harvest Home

How quickly does joy often succeed to sorrow, the day of cheerful hope to that of gloomy fear, and the season of plenty and abundance to that of want and scarcity. At one time the dearth of bread in this land was such, that every countenance seemed to gather blackness; the very heavens also appeared to frown upon us; for the weather, during a long time, was so dismal that it threatened to blast the approaching harvest. Having enjoyed many years of plenty without interruption, we had learned to count upon the continuance of the same blessing; and because God's goodness had been so common, we were so much the less thankful for it.

But let us here endeavor to prevent this forgetfulness of our present mercies in the minds of our readers, and let us invite them to come and contemplate with us that greatness and goodness of our Creator, which are so observable at the time of harvest.

There is, indeed, no part of the creation to which we can turn our eyes without meeting with some proofs of the divine power and mercy. Shall we lift up our eyes to the heavens? There shines the brightness of the sun, which God has placed in the firmament to give light and heat to the world. Shall we wait till the sun is set? Then the moon and the stars take up the same language of praise, and tell of their Maker's power and goodness.

Shall we turn our eyes to the earth? See how the surface of it is spread forth like a carpet, decked with everything to charm the eye, to delight the sense, and to apply the wants of man. Shall we look upon the great and wide ocean? There go the ships; and behold even the sea is filled with food for the use of man. "How manifold are Thy works, O Lord; in wisdom hast Thou made them all."

The sight of these common objects of nature used often to carry out the holy men of old in praise and adoration to God, of which we will mention an instance in the sixty-fifth Psalm, because it is applicable to the present time – a psalm penned after a long drought, to which had succeeded very plentiful and refreshing rains. The psalmist, while he walks abroad, and delights himself with the beautiful appearance of the harvest, and the prospect of plenty which is on every side, breaks out in the following thanksgiving to the bountiful Giver of all things.

"Praise waiteth for Thee, O God, in Zion; and unto Thee shall the vow be performed. O Thou that hearest prayer, unto Thee shall all flesh come." "Thou makest the outgoings of the morning and evening to rejoice. Thou visitest the earth, and watereth it; Thou greatly enrichest it with the river of God" – for the clouds are compared to a river in the air, sustained by the hand of the Almighty – "Thou preparest corn when Thou hast so provided for it. Thou waterest the ridges thereof abundantly; Thou settlest the furrows thereof; Thou makest it soft with showers; Thou blessest the springing thereof. Thou crownest the year with Thy goodness, and Thy paths drop fatness. The little hills rejoice on every side; the pastures are clothed with flocks; the valleys also are covered over with corn; they shout for joy, they also sing."

To every one who is of the same mind with the psalmist, the same kind of meditations will be very apt to occur. Let us, however, here assist the reader by naming a few subjects, which he will do well to reflect upon while he takes his walk amidst the reapers, and admires the plenty that is in the fields.

First, then, how naturally ought the season of harvest to send our thoughts to the great Author of it. How clearly is His hand at this time seen. All the power and ingenuity of the whole world cannot frame so much as a single ear of corn. The part which man has in procuring the corn is very small indeed. He in fact does nothing himself towards its growth; he only places the seed in a situation which from experience he has found to be favorable to it, and then "he goeth away, and it springeth up he knoweth not how." The seed which he plants was in the first place given by God. When the sower has put it into the ground, there is then a work or operation carried on, in which man is not only unconcerned, but he does not even know how it is accomplished. The grain dies, and from that death a resurrection takes place, a fresh plant arises out of the ground; and this plant is nourished by means of roots hidden within the earth, which then shoot forth without the aid of man. In this secret manner are the different juices collected and sent through the plant; by and by the flower blooms; the ear forms itself, and the corn takes the proper shape and substance; the rain in the meantime waters it, the dews descend, and the sun shines upon it, till at length it is fit for the use of man. In all this, man can do nothing. It is during his absence even that this work is going on. If the grain is blighted, man cannot help it; if it grows too slowly, he is not able to quicken it; he can only look on with hope and fear, and watch it in its different stages; he must ascribe all its growth to the unassisted power of the great Creator of all things.

Plain as the hand of the Creator is in the production of the corn, yet such is our natural ignorance, that while we gather the corn, we often think no more of God in it, than the very cattle which draw it home. The farmer speaks of his own skill, and labor, and pains; and when the grain is ripe, he lays it up in his barn with much self-applause, and begins to count his gains, not considering that all the praise, in fact, is due to God, and that every ear which is laid up is a proof of man's obligation to his Maker.

But let us here notice also the largeness of the divine bounty. The works of God are upon a large scale; they are like Himself, infinite. The works of man are little and insignificant; it is but a small spot which his strength can water; but the showers of Heaven water a whole territory at once. It is but a few acres which the diligent labors of man can make productive; but God causes His sun to shine, and His dew to descend, and the whole earth is rendered fruitful. Look over that beautiful and extensive prospect; see as far as the eye can reach how the fields are crowned with plenty; extend the scene in your imagination – still the same rich view of the divine bounty presents itself. Cross the wide ocean, and survey the different countries of which the earth consists. In all the varied productions of these different climates, we only meet with more signs of the divine goodness. How are we then called upon to admire and adore that glorious Being, who suffers no part of the earth to escape His kind and beneficial notice!

With the extensiveness of this bounty, let the continuance of it be considered. No sooner is the harvest got in, than again the seed is committed to the ground, and again the same scene returns upon us. Let us carry back our thoughts to the years that have been of old. How unwearied has been our great Benefactor. How unceasing the exertions of His goodness. How many generations have been fed and supported by it. Seasons have changed, but they have only presented different views of the Lord's mercy, and the cold of winter, the bloom of spring, the heat of summer, and the fruits of autumn, have each in its season manifested the same bounty and care of our Creator.

Having indulged in these pleasing reflections upon the divine bounty, it seems proper in the next place to turn our attention to a more melancholy subject – I mean, our unworthiness of it. For whom does the Lord open His store, and provide with so liberal a hand? For a race of creatures who are touched with the most lively sense of His goodness, and love and honor Him in proportion to these great obligations?

Do we then hear the reapers, while they cut down the corn, speaking good of the name of the Lord, and blessing Him for His kindness to the children of men? Hark! Is it hymns of praise which they are chanting in yonder field? Is the song they sing the song of the psalmist which has just been spoken of? I think, instead of it, some song of profaneness and obscenity is sung aloud. The name of God, indeed, is on many lips, but it is only that it may be trifled with or blasphemed. What then, are these men gathering God's bounty, and in the same moment profaning His name? But follow them to the harvest home; surely now, we may suppose, they meet and offer up their prayer and thanksgiving; and while God is in the act of crowning the year with His bounty, each tongue is loud in talking of His mercy, and each grateful heart is swelling with His praise. But it is commonly reported, that there is no season of the year in which so much wickedness and drunkenness prevail among the farmers, as in that of bringing the harvest home. Are these, then, the returns which in this year also we are making to the divine goodness? Is all our complaining of want, and our prayer to God for deliverance, to end in a drunken abuse of the mercies He so wonderfully bestows?

But not to dwell on vices which are so great that we would willingly hope they must only be the vices of a few, let us a little consider also the general unworthiness of mankind. Who are they that will be fed by this abundant harvest? Will no idle persons be maintained by it? Will no sinners have their strength sustained, so as to continue their life of sin? Will there be none who will eat it with unthankfulness? None who, as the reapers have reaped it without thinking of the Author of the harvest, will in like manner feed upon it without thinking of the Author of their food? Again, will no discontented, murmuring, repining people be fed by the goodness of the Lord? Will all those, in short, whose life is prolonged by the bread now sent them, devote that life to the service of Him who prolonged it?

Surely, if we could remove ourselves to a distance from the earth, and become by any means impartial judges between God and man, we should stand astonished at the present rebellion of the creature. He who made man, He who supports him, sending him the very bread which he eats, has a right to his services, and hath made him, no doubt, for His own glory. I think, if any of us were endowed with power to create some little rational animal inferior to ourselves, and if, after having breathed into him the breath of life, we also daily clothed and nourished him, we should expect his obedience and constant service in return. And if, after all, such a being should presume to set up for himself, and pretend to have a will of his own, and break all the laws we had given him, we should be ready, I think, to stamp our foot upon him, and to crush him to death at once for not fulfilling the ends of his creation. We should have no patience with such a little insolent and rebellious animal. And yet God has patience with us, notwithstanding all our forgetfulness of the ends for which we were born, and our unthankfulness for the daily returns of His bounty. Nay, though we go on abusing His mercies, He goes on clothing the pastures with His flocks. The valleys also are again covered over with corn; again they shout for joy, they also sing. O let us be ashamed of the baseness of our ingratitude, and repent in the name of Christ, before the day of His vengeance comes upon us.

The season of harvest is also one which should lead us particularly to reflect on our dependence upon God. God gave us life at first. He causes our blood to flow, our heart to beat, and our stomach to distribute the nourishment. He too, supplies the food we eat, of whatever kind it be. We may combine together different meats, we may dress them in a variety of ways, but we can create nothing. God is the only Giver of life, and food, and all things; and happy is that man who lives in the lively remembrance of this, who accepts all his comforts as from the hand of the great God – habitually feeling that he has not of himself power to exist for a single moment, or to procure independently of God one single drop of water, or grain of bread. And this sense of our dependence is not a duty only, it is a great comfort also; for how does it tend to relieve all that anxiety which is so natural to us about our existence in the time to come. The more we remember that we are the creatures of God, so much the more shall we trust in Him to provide for His large family, even as a child trusts to the care and prudence of his parent. "Behold the fowls of the air; they sow not, neither do they reap, nor gather into barns, yet your heavenly Father feedeth them."

Next to this sense of our dependence, gratitude to God may be mentioned as peculiarly becoming. I think, at this time, not only the heavens above, but the earth beneath, calls aloud upon us to be thankful. Every field, every ear of corn, seems to bid us speak the praises of God. How do these glorify Him, as it were, by an expressive though dumb offering of praise! But man has a tongue with which he can speak forth the praises of his Maker. It is for the sake of man also, that the storehouse of divine bounty is opened; it is for man that the pastures are clothed with flocks, and the valleys covered with corn; it is for man that the sun shines, and the showers descend. From Him, then, should the offering of praise continually ascend.

"But why will you suppose mankind to be so unthankful?" I think I hear some one reply. "Do you think we do not know as well as you that we ought to praise God for a good harvest? There will always, indeed, be a few wicked people in the land, but in general we understand well enough that it is God who sends us bread, and all our mercies; when any of us speak of having a good crop, 'Thank God' is the very phrase that is quite common in our lips."

I admit it is so; and I hope, indeed, that many thousand hearts have already offered up the sincere tribute of thanksgiving for the present plentiful season. But we cannot help adding here, that there is a way far beyond that of simple praise, by which true gratitude will manifest itself. It will break out not in words only, but in deeds – in deeds of obedience to Him towards whom the gratitude is felt. What would any father think of the gratitude of a child, or any husband of the gratitude of a wife, which never showed itself in any thing else but a few warm expressions of obligation? No, it is by the readiness and activity in serving the person praised, and by the desire in all respects to please him, that the disposition to gratitude must be judged of. A man may say, "Thank God," twenty times a day, and yet never truly thank Him in his heart. Words are cheap. Many men think to pay God off, as it were, by this sort of coin.

Let it be remarked, also, that there is a satisfaction and self-complacency which are naturally felt on receiving an abundance of wealth into our lap. We are put into a good humor by it, and when we are reminded that God is the Author of our prosperity, the truth of this is so plain that we cannot deny it; and since our understandings agree to the observation, we fancy that our hearts agree also; whereas, in fact, we only judge that God ought to be thanked, but we do not thank Him; and as to the good humor we are in, it arises merely from our being well pleased with ourselves, or with the enjoyments which God has given us, and not from our being well pleased with God. That we practice some such frauds as these in ourselves is but too plain; for mark now what follows.

When the same person who has been thanking God so often for His mercies, is by and by called to do something, to suffer something, or to give up something for the sake of serving this gracious Being to whom he professed such great gratitude, he is then either too idle, or too selfish, or too much governed by the opinion of his fellow-creatures, or some way or other too full of excuses to do what is wanted of him. On the other hand, when some temptation comes in his way he yields to it, and sins against the same God as freely as if he were under no obligation to Him. Let us then beware of this hypocritical sort of gratitude, by which we cannot deceive God, though we often delude ourselves by it. Let us show forth His praise not only with our lips, but with our lives. Let us show our sense of His goodness by doing His will, by reading His Word, by attending His worship, by readily denying ourselves for His sake, and in short, by laying out our lives in His service, and by standing forth to promote His cause in a disobedient and unthankful world.

Here let it be hinted, also, that this may be a good time for laying down our plans for using the plenty which is flowing in to us. God has now given us provision for another year, but for what purpose has He given it? In order that we may eat, and drink, and be merry? What then, have we not immortal souls? The great end of our Creator is, that we may serve Him in this world, and may be prepared to dwell with Him forever in Heaven. His direction is, that we should employ our health and strength, and all our vigor of body and mind, in fulfilling His will; that we should seek, in the first place, to know God, and Jesus Christ, whom He has sent into the world; and having learned to know Him, that we should then act in our several stations from love to His name, imitating all His bounty, by ministering to the necessities of our fellow-creatures. Are these then our ends of living? Is this what we propose to ourselves? Are these the views with which we reap the harvest? Are we determined that none of it, as far as in us lies, shall be wasted in riot, or in luxury, or in imprudent consumption? Do we look forward to it as to a treasure, with which the hungry shall be fed, and the poor satisfied? Then, indeed, we may rejoice in the bounty of Heaven, and may reasonably trust that all the expressions of gratitude on our lips are sincere.

Again, let the consideration of the goodness of God, displayed in the fruits of the earth, raise our minds to the contemplation of those still greater mercies which He is able and willing to give us. It is with Him a small matter to provide the earth with food, or to take care of the body. See what rich provision He has made for our souls – for them He has not spared His only begotten Son, but given Him up to be the propitiation for our sins. For the sake of the soul, He has sent His Holy Spirit into the world, to guide men into the knowledge of the truth. For the souls He has prepared an eternal harvest of blessings, "an inheritance which is incorruptible, undefiled, and that fadeth not away, reserved in Heaven for us."

We may learn to value spiritual mercies from what we see of temporal ones. Temporal ones strike the senses, and being suited to our present fallen nature, are more apt to fill our hearts with joy and gratitude. But we may rest assured that the blessings which God hath provided for the soul, are as much superior to those provided for the body, as the soul is to the body, and as eternity is to time. Let us then turn from this earthly scene of abundance to still nobler and larger blessings. Let the fields not only preach to us the immense goodness of our Creator, but let them send our thoughts also to the "unsearchable riches that are in Christ." Let the harvest serve to impress a thoughtless world with wonder, gratitude, reverence, and love to Him who is the Author, not of all our earthly treasures only, but of all the blessings of eternity. In short, let the goodness of God lead us all to repentance, and let

A HYMN OF PRAISE

FOR THE ABUNDANT HARVEST OF 1796
AFTER A YEAR OF SCARCITY

Great God, when famine threatened late
To scourge our guilty land,
O did we learn from that dark fate,
To dread Thy mighty hand?

Did then our sins to memory rise,
Or owned we God was just?
Or raised we penitential cries,
Or bowed we in the dust?

Did we forsake one evil path;
Was any sin abhorred?
Or did we prevent Thy wrath,
Thus to turn us to the Lord?

'Tis true, we failed not to repine,
But did we too repent,
Or own the chastisement divine,
In awful judgment sent?

Though the bright chain of peace is broke,
And war with ruthless sword
Unpeoples nations at a stroke,
Yet who regards the Lord?

But God, who in His strict decrees
Remembers mercy still,
Can in a moment, if He please,
Our hearts with comfort fill.

He marked our angry spirits rise,
Domestic hate increase,
And for a time withheld supplies,
To teach us love and peace.

He, when He brings His children low,
Has blessings still in store;
And when He strikes the heaviest blow,
He does but love us more.

Now frost, and flood, and blight no more
Our golden harvests spoil,
See what an unexampled store
Rewards the reapers' toil.

As when the promised harvest failed
In Canaan's fruitful land,
The envious patriarchs were assailed
By famine's pressing hand.

The angry brothers then forgot
Each fierce and jarring feud,
United by their adverse lot,
They loved as brothers should.

So here, from Heaven's correcting hand,
Though famine failed to move,
Let plenty now throughout the land
Rekindle peace and love.

Like the rich fool, let us not say,
Soul, thou hast goods in store;
But shake the overplus away,
To feed the aged poor.

Let rich and poor, on whom are now
Such bounteous crops bestowed,
Raise many a pure and holy vow
In gratitude to God.

And while His gracious name we praise,
For bread so kindly given,
Let us beseech Him all our days,
To give the Bread of Heaven.

In that blest prayer our Lord did frame,
Of all our prayers the guide,
We ask the "hallowed be His name,"
And then our needs supplied.

For grace He bids us first implore,
Next, that we may be fed;
We say, "Thy will be done," before
We ask "our daily bread."